Mallory
on the
Move

Absolutely, Positively, 100% for David

—L. F.

For Olivia

—T. S.

Text copyright © 2004 by Laurie B. Friedman
Illustrations copyright © 2004 by Tamara Schmitz

Carolrhoda Books
A division of Lerner Publishing Group, Inc.
241 First Avenue North
Minneapolis, MN 55401 U.S.A.

Website address: www.lernerbooks.com

Library of Congress Cataloging-in-Publication Data

Friedman, Laurie B.
  Mallory on the move / by Laurie B. Friedman ; illustrations by Tamara Schmitz.
    p. cm.
  Summary: After moving to a new town, eight-year-old Mallory keeps throwing stones in the "Wishing Pond" but things will not go back to the way they were before, and she remains torn between old and new best friends.
  ISBN-13: 978-1-57505-538-1 (lib. bdg. : alk. paper)
  ISBN-10: 1-57505-538-4 (lib. bdg. : alk. paper)
  [1. Moving, Household—Fiction. 2. Best friends—Fiction. 3 . Friendship—Fiction. 4. Wishes—Fiction. 5. Family life—Fiction.] I. Schmitz, Tamara, ill. II. Title.
  PZ7.F89773Mal 2004
  [Fic]—dc21
                                                                    2003008937

Manufactured in the United States of America
7 8 9 10 11 12 — BP — 13 12 11 10 09 08

Mallory
on the
Move

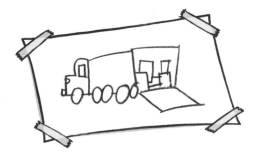

by Laurie Friedman

illustrations by Tamara Schmitz

Carolrhoda Books   minneapolis • New York

CONTENTS

A WORD FROM MALLORY

moving is a big deal!

When you move, everything changes: your house, your neighborhood, your town, and, worst of all, your friends.

And no one asks if you want to move. It would be nice if your parents said: "Hey, we're thinking about moving. That means you'll have to get used to a new house in a new neighborhood in a new town. You'll have to make all new friends. But we won't do it unless it's OK with you. What do you say?"

Nope. That's not how it happens at all.

First, your parents start whispering to each other.

Then, they have lots of conversations behind closed doors.

Finally, the big day comes. Your parents tell you to sit down. They have an announcement to make. You're moving! And as fast as you can snap your fingers, it's all been decided for you.

I know. I'm Mallory McDonald (like the restaurant but no relation). Age 8 1/2 plus 1 month. And that's exactly what happened to me.

When my parents told me I had to move, I asked if they were joking. Everybody knows I love a good joke. But I knew with one look, it was no joke.

And then I got mad. REALLY MAD!

"You ruined my life!" I screamed at my parents. "I'm not moving, and if you try to make me, I'm running away from home!"

Mom told me that running away from home was the same thing as moving, except you have to cook all your own meals. I don't know how to cook.

That's when I knew I was stuck moving.

PACKING

My room is filled with boxes.

Yesterday it was filled with stuffed animals and books and posters. Today it is filled with boxes that are filled with stuffed animals and books and posters.

I'm supposed to be filling more boxes with my stuff. But I don't get it. If I don't want to move, how come I'm stuck packing?

What I need is a helper. I yell from the top of the stairs.

"Mom!"

I wait for an answer. But I don't get one so I use my outdoor voice.

"MOM!"

She comes to the bottom of the stairs with an armload of boxes.

"Hey, Mom, what's big and brown and empty?"

"Mallory, I don't have time for jokes," Mom says. "We have to pack. We're moving in two days."

"I know. But what's big and brown and empty?"

Mom blows a piece of hair out of her mouth. "What?"

"The boxes in my room!" I laugh out loud.

"Mallory, that's about as funny as an overflowing toilet."

I happen to think an overflowing toilet is

hilarious. But I can see Mom doesn't.

"Please go pack," she says.

"But I don't want to move to Fern Falls." I whimper like a sad, cold puppy left outside in the rain.

Mom looks at me like she can't decide what to do. Then she puts her boxes down and walks up the stairs. "Cheer up." She pats me on the head. "I'll help."

I sit on the bed with my cat, Cheeseburger. We watch Mom take T-shirts and shorts from my drawers. She folds them neatly and puts them in a big box. When the box is full, she tapes it shut and writes Mallory's T-shirts and shorts on the outside with a fat purple marker.

I think over the plan Mary Ann and I came up with: *Operation-Convince-My-Mom-that-Moving-and-Leaving-Behind-My-Best-Friend-Is-a-Bad-Idea.*

Mom starts folding a pile of blue jeans.

I pull a clipboard and a pencil out of the drawer in my night table. "Mom, I have something I need to discuss with you."

She stops folding.

I cross my toes. I hope this works.

"Mary Ann and I have been planning this summer for a long time. We have a very busy schedule." I read from my clipboard.

"Mondays: paint toenails and cat claws.

"Tuesdays: bake cookies and cat treats."

I smile at Mom. I don't tell her we'll need her help with the oven on Tuesdays.

"Wednesdays: work on our summer scrapbook.

"Thursdays: go swimming!"

I remember what Mary Ann told me. Just read the list. I don't mention to Mom that before we go swimming, we need to go bathing suit shopping.

Mary Ann said the best time to mention the bathing suit thing is on the way to the swimming pool.

"Fridays: sleepover at Mary Ann's house.

"Saturdays: sleepover at my house.

"Sundays: watch movies in our pajamas all day."

I look up from my clipboard. Mom looks like she swallowed an olive.

I can't tell if that's a good sign or a bad sign. "As you can see from this very busy schedule, I don't have time to move this summer." I shrug my shoulders. "Sorry. Maybe we can talk again in the fall."

"Mallory . . ." Mom starts to say something. But I don't let her get too far. I can see the plan isn't working like Mary Ann and I thought it would. I switch to Plan B.

"Mom, have you thought this through?" I try to stay calm, but my voice sounds like

it's starting to get upset. "What about your students?"

"There are plenty of good piano teachers in town." Mom folds a pair of jeans across her lap.

"Please!" I get down on my hands and knees. "Please, please, please, please, can we please not move?"

Mom puts the jeans in a box. "Mallory, how many times do we have to go over this?"

My brother, Max, comes in my room and sits down on my dresser. "Somewhere between a hundred and a thousand is my guess," he says. "She's kind of thick for a kid her age. If you know what I mean."

Max thinks he's so smart just because he's ten. I get up off the floor and try pulling him by his feet to get him off my dresser. "Mom!" I moan. "Do something!"

But she can't. Her head is inside a box.

Max tosses a baseball in the air and catches it without looking. "It's simple," he says. "We're moving because Dad is opening a new store in Fern Falls."

"Simple for you," I say. "You don't care where you live. All you care about is baseball. You'll find a new team. It's a lot harder to find a new best friend."

"You're lucky," says Max. "You won't have to be best friends with Birdbrain anymore."

I know Max is talking about Mary Ann. We've lived next door to each other since we were born, and we do everything together.. We go to the same school. We chew the same kind of gum. We even paint our toenails the same color.

I cross my arms across my chest. "Mary Ann has been my best friend forever, and I want to keep it that way."

"You might miss Mary Ann," says Max. "But I sure won't."

Mom takes her head out of the box. "Max, please go get more tape."

"I'm not moving to Fern Falls," I tell her when Max is gone.

I sit down on the box Mom is packing. "You and Dad and Max can go. I'll stay here and live with Mary Ann. She said her mom will be glad to have the company since it's just the two of them now."

Mom sits down on the box next to me. "I know you don't want to leave Mary Ann.

And I know she's had a hard time since her parents' divorce. But you'll make new friends. And so will she."

Mom picks up my hand and squeezes it. "Don't forget, Mary Ann can come visit. Fern Falls is only three hours away."

Max comes back in my room and tosses the tape to Mom. "No visits! Please! I've been waiting my entire life to get away from Birdbrain. My wish is finally coming true. Don't ruin it now."

"Max, that's enough." Mom puts her arm around me and pulls me toward her. "Why don't you tell me your joke about the laughing cow?"

"Maybe some other time," I tell her.

It's a funny joke. But moving is no laughing matter.

BLUE WITHOUT YOU

"Rise and shine, Sweet Potato."

I feel someone sit down on my bed. I don't have to open my eyes to know it's Mom. She's the only one who calls me Sweet Potato.

"Knock, knock," I mumble.

"Who's there?" she says.

"Leaf."

"Leaf who?"

"Leaf me alone. . . . I WANT TO SLEEP!" I groan. "Five more minutes."

"We have to finish packing," says Mom.

I roll over and pull the covers over my face. But Mom sticks her head under so she can see me. "Did you forget what's happening today?"

My party! Mary Ann is giving a good-bye party for me. Lots of kids are coming. She told them all to bring presents. I hop out of bed. Now I'm ready to pack!

Mom hands me a list, and we start filling boxes. Sweaters. Socks. Underwear. I check things off the list as we go. Snow boots. Scrapbooks. Bead collection.

My room looks more like a warehouse than a bedroom.

When the phone rings, I run down the hall. "I'll get it!" I yell over my shoulder.

Anything is better than packing.

"Hello," I say.

"Hey, hey, hey," says a familiar voice. "Can you come over now? It's almost time for the party."

"I'll be right over."

I race back to my room. "Mom, can I go to Mary Ann's now? Please? Please? Please?"

Mom smiles and tells me to have fun, fun, fun.

I walk next door with Cheeseburger and knock on Mary Ann's window. She opens it

just a crack. "Password, please."

I whisper through the crack.

Mary Ann flings opens her window, and Cheeseburger and I climb inside. She gives me a big hug and Cheeseburger a little hug. "I'm so, so, so sad today is your last day."

Mary Ann and I always say things three times. It was Mary Ann's idea. She says it shows we've got style.

Mary Ann puts her box of polishes on the floor. "Want to paint our toenails for the party?"

"Purple?" I say. Purple is our favorite color.

"Not today." Mary Ann picks out a bottle of baby blue polish. "Today is blue day."

While we're painting, Max sticks his head in the window. "Hey, Birdbrain, don't even think about planning any visits."

"If I make any visits, it won't be to see

you!" Mary Ann gets up and shuts her window.

"Ready for the party?" she says.

She must be kidding. She knows I can't wait!

Mary Ann puts her hands over my eyes. "OK. No peeking." She walks me down the hall.

I can't see a thing. When she moves her hands, I rub my eyes. Everything in her living room is blue!

There are blue streamers and blue balloons hanging from the ceiling. There is a blue table cloth on the table and blue plates and cups and napkins.

Even the food is blue. Little bowls of blue Jell-O and blue M&Ms and blue jelly beans on the pizza.

There's a big sign hanging over the fireplace. We'll be BLUE without you!

"Wow!" I say. "It's hard to feel BLUE when I'm with you!" But I do feel blue. I know tomorrow I won't be with Mary Ann anymore.

Mary Ann's mom tells Mary Ann and me to get together. We put our arms around each other, and she snaps our picture. "We'll send you one for the scrapbook," she says.

The doorbell rings, and Mary Ann opens the door. The guests begin to arrive. They all have on blue T-shirts.

We eat pizza. Then Mary Ann says, "Does anyone have anything for Mallory?"

Becca Birdwell gives me an address book. "So you won't forget us when you move." She writes her address in the book and passes it around the room.

Claudia Thompson gives me a cat-of-the-month calendar. Everybody knows I love cats.

Emily and Ellen Edwards give me a candle that looks like a cheeseburger. There are layers of lettuce and pickles and tomatoes. There's even a meat and a bun layer. It looks so real I could eat it.

"Open mine," says Stephanie Sanders. She gives me a joke book.

I flip through the pages and stop at the section with cat jokes. I pick up Cheeseburger and cover her ears. "What do you call a mad cat?"

No one knows.

"A crabby tabby!

Everybody laughs.

I read another one. "What do you call a fat cat?"

I pause. "A flabby tabby."

"Funny! Funny! Funny!" says Mary Ann. Then she hands me another box. It's wrapped in purple paper with a purple bow. "From me," she says.

I tear the paper off slowly. I lift the lid off a small box. Inside are two bottles of light purple glitter polish. I read the card.

Roses are red and violets are blue.
One is for me and one is for you.

Mary Ann takes one of the bottles of polish out of the box and stuffs it in her pocket. "No matter where we live, our toes will always match."

I hug Mary Ann and promise never to wear anything else.

When Mom comes to get me, Mary Ann's mom asks about the family that bought our house.

"They have a son who's eight," Mom tells her.

"Perfect," says Mary Ann's mom. "There will be somebody on the street for Mary Ann to play with."

Mary Ann leans over and grabs her stomach. "Me! Play with a boy! I'm going to be sick, sick, sick!"

Everyone laughs except Mary Ann's mom. "I'm sure he's nice," she says.

"Time to say good-bye," my mom says.

Now I'm the one who feels sick. And I don't think it's from the M&Ms or the jelly beans on the pizza. I hug everybody, but I save Mary Ann for last.

When I hug her, she raises her pinkie on her right hand. "Let's pinkie swear." I hook my pinkie around hers.

"I pinkie swear I won't be friends with the boy next door," says Mary Ann.

Since I won't live here anymore, it doesn't make sense for me to pinkie swear that. But I have to promise something.

"I pinkie swear I'll never be friends with any boy next door."

Then we squeeze our pinkies together, and it's official.

I sure am going to miss Mary Ann.

WISH POND ROAD

I press a button on the side of my watch, and the face lights up. It's only 8:30 in the morning, and we've been driving for two hours.

I feel sick. The problem is I don't know if I'm carsick or moving sick. I clutch my stomach and lean over the front seat. "How much longer?" I moan.

"An hour," says Dad.

"Quiet," grumbles Max. He stretches and puts his feet on my side of the seat. "I'm trying to sleep."

I hold my nose and push Max's stinky feet back to his side of the car. I don't see how Max can even think about sleeping on a day like today.

We're moving, and my brain is filled with questions. I tap Dad on the shoulder. "Tell me why our street is named Wish Pond Road?"

Dad smiles at me in the rearview mirror. "Do you want to hear the Legend of the Wish Pond?"

Dad already told me this story, but I'm having a hard time deciding if I think it's true.

I shrug. I don't want Dad to get the wrong idea and think I'm excited about moving to a street named Wish Pond Road.

I do want to hear the story again.

Dad clears his throat. "Legend has it that many years ago, a farmer and his wife lived on a large and beautiful farm right where our street is now."

"What did they have on their farm?" I ask.

"Good question," says Dad. "They had just about everything a farmer and his wife could want. They had cows and pigs and chickens and goats. They had corn and

barley and wheat and hay.

"The only thing they didn't have that they wanted were children."

"How sad," says Mom.

"Yes," Dad says. "This made the farmer and his wife very sad indeed. Sometimes while the farmer was out tending to the cows and pigs and chickens and goats, the farmer's wife would go sit by herself on the edge of a small pond in the middle of the farm.

"One day she picked up a rock, threw it into the pond, and made a wish. I wish I had a little boy or a little girl to sit next to me by this pond.

"And to her amazement, her wish came true. The farmer's wife was blessed with a baby boy."

Max stretches across the backseat. "Lucky for her she got a boy."

I roll my eyes at Max. "I bet once he was old enough to talk she wished she could turn him into a girl."

"Quiet, you two, and let me finish the story," says Dad.

"The farmer's wife thought it was possible that her good fortune had come from throwing the rock into the pond," continues Dad. "So she threw another rock into the pond and again wished for a child. This time she and the farmer were blessed with a beautiful baby girl."

I grin at Max.

Dad keeps talking. "Now certain that the pond had magical powers, the farmer's wife decided to make one more wish. She threw another rock into the pond and this time, as was her wish, she was blessed with twins."

"Boys or girls?" I ask Dad.

"I don't really know," says Dad. "And I

don't think it matters. The story is that the farmer and his wife and their children lived long and happy lives on the farm."

"That was a long time ago," continues Dad. "Now the farm is gone, but the pond is still there. And those who know it believe it is a wish pond and that anyone who lives on this street can make three wishes, and they'll come true."

Dad stops his story. I sit quietly for a few minutes. There's something I've wanted to ask him since the first time I heard this story.

"Dad, how do you know the wish pond works?"

He smiles at me in the mirror. "I don't know if it works. We'll have to try it and see. But I think the question you have to ask yourself is if you believe in magic."

Cheeseburger stretches across my lap. I

hope the wish pond works. There are lots
of things I've been wishing for lately. Like
having someone to play with on our new
street.

I rub Cheeseburger's back. "Hey, Dad,
do any kids live on Wish Pond Road?"

"I saw some kids outside playing when I
went to check on the house last week."

I cross my fingers. "Did you see any
eight-year-old girls who looked like they
didn't have a best friend?"

Max sits up. "Did any of them have
wings and feathers and a head the size of a
peanut? If so, they'd make a perfect friend
for Mallory."

I glare at Max. "The first thing I'm going
to do when we get to Wish Pond Road is
throw a rock in the wish pond and wish for
a different brother."

Max takes a doughnut out of a bag. He

shoves it in his mouth and gets crumbs all over his shirt. "You actually believe in magic?"

I look at the mess he's made. "So?"

Max shoves in another doughnut. "So, you would."

Now there are crumbs all over the backseat. "What's that supposed to mean?"

Max looks at me like he can't believe I don't know what he's talking about. "It means you're always doing dumb things, and believing in a magic wish pond is just another dumb thing."

"Max, be nice!" Mom gives him a *close-your-mouth* look.

But Max ignores it. "It's true," he says. "Remember when she tried to fly, and the whole neighborhood saw her do it?"

I'll never forget the day Mary Ann and I

tried to fly. We taped garbage bags to our arms and skated down the hill. Our plan was for the garbage bags to fill with air and lift us off the ground when we flapped our arms. Only too bad for us. . . the plan didn't work like we thought it would.

"Big deal," I say to Max. "I bet a lot of kids wish they could fly like birds."

"Yeah." Max pops another doughnut in his mouth. "But most kids know the difference between birds and humans."

I pick powdered sugar crumbs off my side of the seat. I bet most birds are neater eaters than my brother.

I lean over the seat and shake Mom's shoulder. "Hey, Mom, what's sitting in the backseat and looks like it got lost in a snowstorm?"

"What?" Mom turns around.

"Max! Messy Max!" I laugh so hard my

face hurts.

Mom tells Max to wipe his mouth and brush the powdered sugar off his shirt.

"Don't worry about me," says Max.

"Just look at the backseat," I say.

But Max looks right at me. "You messed up things in our old neighborhood. Try not to do it in the new neighborhood, too."

"I'm not going to mess up anything!" I shout.

"That's enough!" says Dad. He turns the car onto a small street.

A sign says Wish Pond Road. Neat rows of two-story white houses with green shutters and black front doors line both sides of the street.

Dad pulls the car into a driveway of a two-story white house with green shutters and a black front door. "We're here," he says. "Number 17 Wish Pond Road."

I get out of the car and look at my new house. It looks like all the other houses on the street.

I think about the farmer's wife and the pond and how her wishes came true. Then I close my eyes and make a wish.

I wish I didn't have to move into a white house with green shutters and a black door on a street called Wish Pond Road.

I hope my wish comes true. But if it doesn't, I hope I don't get confused and go into the wrong house.

THE GIRL
NEXT DOOR

"Time for the official McDonald family tour," says Dad. He pushes open the front door to 17 Wish Pond Road, and we follow him inside.

First he shows us the family room.

Then the living room.

Then the dining room.

Then the laundry room.

I yawn. The only thing official about this tour is that it's officially boring.

"Now for the bedrooms," says Dad. He leads us into a bedroom downstairs.

"WOW!" Max and I say at the same time. This tour just got interesting!

This room's so big you could fit an elephant into it! I can't wait to call Mary Ann and tell her about my new room.

"Max, this is your room," says Dad. "Follow me. I'll show you Mallory's." We walk through a bathroom. "You two have to share," he says.

Max makes a face like he's going to puke. I don't want to share a bathroom with him either, but I can't wait to see my room.

Dad takes us into another bedroom. It looks like Max's room. But there's one big difference: It's tiny.

"This is a room for a mouse!" I say. "I want the other room."

"Taken," says Max.

"NO FAIR!" I stamp my foot. "Cheeseburger and I have to share a room. This one is too small for both of us."

"Too bad," says Max.

"Mom and I discussed it," says Dad. "It's the only fair way. Max is older."

"DAD!" I give him my *I'm-your-only-daughter* look. I nudge Cheeseburger to give him an *I'm-your-only-cat* look. But neither look does much good.

The doorbell rings. "End of conversation,"

says Dad. He walks out of my room, and I hear him greet the movers.

I look around my room. But it doesn't look like it belongs to me. It just looks like four white walls with none of my stuff on them.

I take my cat-of-the-month calendar out of my backpack and stick it on one of the walls with a pushpin. I pick up Cheeseburger. "Home, not-so-sweet home," I whisper in her ear.

We go outside and sit on the front porch. The movers are taking our stuff off the truck. Everything is wrapped in blankets so it doesn't even look like our stuff.

Then I get a horrible thought. What if it's not? What if the wrong moving truck showed up? What if we got somebody else's stuff, and they get all of ours?

I put my head down on Cheeseburger. I want to call Mary Ann. But what would I say?

Hi Mary Ann. Guess what? All the houses on my street look alike. I can't even tell which one is mine. My room is so small, I don't think there's enough air in there for Cheeseburger and me to make it through the night. And I'm probably going to have to wear some other kid's clothes because the wrong moving truck showed up with somebody else's stuff.

But I am so, so, so glad we moved.

I decide not to call Mary Ann yet.

A door slams and I jump. A girl in a bathing suit walks out of the house next door and into her front yard.

When she looks over, I wave.

She doesn't wave back. "Maybe she's shy," I whisper in Cheeseburger's ear.

She sits in a lawn chair, props her feet up on an ice chest, and puts on dark glasses and headphones.

The girl next door looks like a movie star. Maybe things on Wish Pond Road won't be so bad after all. I pick up Cheeseburger.

"Let's go introduce ourselves."

I walk up to her chair. "Hi," I say in my friendliest voice.

She doesn't move. Her music is probably so loud, she can't hear me.

I try again. Louder this time. "HI!"

She doesn't move. I tap her on the shoulder and use my outdoor voice.
"HI. I'M MALLORY. I'M MOVING IN NEXT DOOR. YOU CAN PROBABLY TELL BECAUSE OF THE MOVING TRUCK IN MY FRONT YARD."

The girl next door takes off her glasses and looks at me. "You're in my sun."

I move to the other side of her chair. "Hey, hey, hey," I say. "I'm Mallory McDonald. Like the restaurant but no relation."

She takes her headphones off her ears. "Winnie Winston."

"Hey, that is so, so, so cool," I say. "Mallory McDonald. Double 'M'. Winnie Winston. Double 'W'. Get it?"

Winnie looks at me like I sneezed on her. "What I don't get is why you say everything three times? Is something wrong with you?"

I think for a second. I have six mosquito bites on my ankle. But other than that, I'm fine. I shake my head.

"Then why do you say things three times?" asks Winnie. "It's weird."

I start to tell Winnie it's not weird, it's my style. But I decide not to. I might decide to change my style.

"Are you eight?" I ask Winnie. "I'm eight."

Winnie stands up straight in front of me. She looks down at me, but she doesn't have to look too far. She's not much taller than I am. "Do I look like I'm eight?"

I look from the bottom of Winnie's feet to the top of her head. "Sort of. It's hard to tell."

Winnie stands up straighter. "I'm ten.

I'll be eleven in two weeks."

"My brother, Max, is turning eleven, too."

"Big deal." Winnie yawns. "Millions of kids are turning eleven."

I look at Winnie's bathing suit. "Were you going to swim in the wish pond? I can put on my bathing suit and go with you."

Winnie points to a pond at the end of our street. "First of all, that thing isn't a wish pond. Everybody knows it's just a plain old pond. And it's the last place I want to go swimming."

Winnie wraps her towel around her waist and looks at me. "Don't think we're going to be friends just because you live next door."

She puts her sunglasses on and walks back in her house. She doesn't even bother to pick up her chair.

I pick up Cheeseburger. *No problem.* I'll

just go see the wish pond myself.

I carry Cheeseburger to the end of my street. I love my cat, but I really wanted my first trip to the wish pond to be with a new friend.

I sit down with Cheeseburger on a big rock on the edge of the pond.

Maybe Winnie is right. Maybe it is just a plain old pond. But it looks like fun to get your feet wet in here.

I rub Cheeseburger's back. "What do you think of the girl next door?" I ask her. But Cheeseburger doesn't say a word.

I pick up a little rock on the edge of the pond and squeeze it in my hand. *I wish someone nice lived next door to me.* I throw my rock into the water.

I've met the girl next door, and I don't think there's much hope of that wish coming true.

JOKE JUICE

The calendar on my wall tells me something I don't want to know: I've lived here for two whole days, and I still don't have a friend. I sit down at my desk and scratch my head. Then I get out a pencil and make a list.

Things I Need to Make New Friends:
- 1 table
- 1 folding chair
- 1 pitcher of juice
- paper cups

First, I look for a table and folding chair. In my old house, I knew where to look for stuff. I have to look in three closets before I find what I need.

I set up the table and chair in our front yard.

Then, I go into the kitchen and get out a big pitcher. Time to make Joke Juice. The problem is, I've never made it before so I'm not sure what's in it.

I decide to use the 1-2-3-4-5 method.

    One carton orange juice

    Two cans grape soda

    Three cups chocolate milk

    Four teaspoons spaghetti sauce

    Five drops blue food coloring

    Salt

    Pepper

    Stir

I hold the pitcher up to the light and add

more spaghetti sauce. I hope Joke Juice tastes better than it looks.

I take the pitcher outside and put it on the table. Then I go to my room to make a sign. When I'm done, I read it to Cheeseburger.

Meet tHe AMaZiNG
MALLORY
• WatcH heR dRiNK JoKe JuicE
• LisTeN to HeR teLL fuNNy JoKes
COST: FREE!

I hurry outside, tape it to the front of the table, and sit down. All I have to do now is wait.

A boy rides over on a skateboard. A small black dog follows him. It sits when he snaps his fingers. "Hey, I'm Joey," he says. "I live next door."

I read his T-shirt.

*I didn't do it, nobody saw me do it, I think I
need to speak to my lawyer.*

"I'm Mallory, and I've never met a kid
who has his own lawyer."

"My grandpa gave me the shirt." Joey
grins. "He's my lawyer, and he lives with
me."

"You live with your grandpa?"

"And my dad and my sister."

"What about your mom?" I ask Joey.

Joey stops grinning. "She died. So my
grandpa came to live with us."

I feel like someone punched me in the
stomach. I don't know anyone whose mom
died. I can't imagine what it would be like
if my mom died.

"I'm sorry about your mom," I tell Joey.

"It's OK," he says. "It happened a long
time ago."

"Is Winnie your big sister?"

"I don't like to tell people that when I first meet them," says Joey. "But we share the same gene pool. I'm not exactly what you'd call her favorite person."

"I know what you mean." I swat a mosquito off my face. "My brother, Max, feels the same way about me."

I point to Joey's dog. "Is he yours?"

Joey snaps his fingers. "Murphy, shake." Murphy holds up a paw, and I shake it.

I giggle. I'm not used to shaking paws with my neighbors. "How did he learn to shake?"

Joey rubs behind Murphy's ears. "Murphy can do lots of tricks." Joey claps his hands. Murphy lies down on the ground and rolls over.

"Wow!" I pick up Cheeseburger and introduce her to Joey. "I would tell her to shake, but she doesn't know how."

"Maybe we can teach her," says Joey.

Teaching Cheeseburger to do cat tricks sounds like fun. Then I remember my pinkie swear to Mary Ann: *I'll never be friends with any boy next door.* I don't say a word.

"What's Joke Juice?" Joey asks me.

I hold up the pitcher. Showing him how Joke Juice works does not exactly make us friends. "Gross!" he says.

"Magic!" I say. "When I drink it, I'll be able to tell a joke without having to think of one. Want to see?"

Joey nods.

I pour some Joke Juice into a cup. It smells like rotten tomatoes. Ugh! I close my eyes and take a sip. I hope I don't throw up.

I open my eyes and take a deep breath. "What does a raccoon get when it rains?"

"What?" asks Joey.

"Wet!"

"Good one." Joey laughs.

"Want to hear another one?" I take a sip of Joke Juice. I'm ready to tell my joke when Winnie walks over to my stand. "What's Joke Juice?"

I start to explain, but Winnie interrupts me. "Yeah, I can read. So let's hear a joke."

"How do you make a Dalmatian disappear?"

Winnie puts her hands on her hips. "How?"

"Spot remover!"

"Great joke!" Joey slaps his forehead.

Winnie rolls her eyes. "First of all, that's not what you use

spot remover for. And second of all, you don't need special juice to tell a joke that dumb."

My stomach feels funny. Maybe it's from the Joke Juice. "Watch again." I take another sip. "What do you call a stupid skeleton?"

"What?" asks Winnie.

"A bonehead."

Joey cracks up. Winnie stares at me. "Are you as good at spelling as you are at telling jokes?"

I'm a pretty good speller. I nod my head.

"Do you know what this word spells? B-O-R-I-N-G." Winnie stretches and pretends to yawn.

"What's going on?" Max comes outside and reads my sign.

"Do you know the amazing Mallory?" Winnie asks.

Max looks at Winnie like she's Miss America. Then he looks at me like I'm a leftover pickle. "I'm not in the mood for jokes," he says. He grabs my sign and my arm and drags me toward the front door.

"I'll be right back," I tell Joey and Winnie. "Careful with that sign," I tell Max. "I was just starting to make friends."

Max squeezes my arm. "Mom! Dad!" he yells when we're inside.

"What's wrong?" Mom rushes into the living room. Dad is right behind her.

"The Amazing Mallory has done it again." Max shoves my sign in Mom's face. "She's the laughingstock of Wish Pond Road and not because she tells funny jokes."

Mom and Dad read my sign.

Dad smiles.

"C'mon, Max," says Mom. "Mallory is just trying to make some new friends."

Max starts to say more, but I don't stay to listen. I run into my room and slam the door. I get it. The only joke here is me.

A PHONE CALL

"Which McDonald wants McDonald's tonight?" Dad grabs his car keys off the counter. He knows McDonald's is my favorite. I think he feels sorry for me because Max thought Joke Juice was a neighborhood joke.

"Last one in is a rotten egg," Dad says on his way out the door. Max is right behind him.

I try to catch up. But I can't. I have to waddle like a duck because my toenails are wet.

"Quack! Quack!" Max laughs as he passes me.

I ignore him. I don't want to mess up my polish.

On my way out the door, the phone rings. "I'll get it!" I waddle back over and pick it up.

"Hey, hey, hey!" says a voice on the other end.

It's Mary Ann! It's so great to hear her voice.

I plop down on the couch and wiggle my toes. They sparkle in the light. "Hey, hey, hey," I say.

"I have a surprise for you!" Mary Ann squeals so loudly I have to hold the phone away from my ear.

"Tell me! Tell me! Tell me!" I squeal back. I love surprises, and I'm going to pop if she doesn't spit this one out fast.

"I'M COMING TO VISIT!"

This is an amazing surprise.

"AWESOME! AWESOME! AWESOME!" I say. "We're going to have so much fun. We can even make a scrapbook of your visit."

I start to tell her all the fun things we can do when she's here. But I don't get too far.

"C'mon," Max yells from the front door. "We're waiting, and I'm starving."

I ignore Max. All he ever thinks about is baseball and what he's going to put in his stomach.

"When are you coming?" I ask Mary Ann. I don't think I can wait another day.

"In one month," she says. "Mom said she will drive me down, and we can stay for the weekend. ONE WHOLE WEEKEND!" she says.

But all I can think is: ONE WHOLE MONTH!

This is not totally awesome. This is totally terrible. How am I going to wait one whole month for Mary Ann to come visit?

"Get a move on," Max shouts from the door.

"I have to go," I tell Mary Ann. "But I promise to write."

"I promise to write you back," says Mary Ann.

"Bye, bye, bye." I pretend to cry into the phone.

"Bye, bye, bye." Mary Ann pretends to cry back.

I announce my surprise when I get into the car. "Mary Ann is coming to visit!"

Mom and Dad smile at each other. They don't seem surprised at all. But Max seems real surprised.

"Birdbrain is coming to Fern Falls!" He rolls down his window and leans his head out. "Help, I need air."

"Max!" Mom gives him a *don't-get-started* look. Dad points to a baseball field. "That's where you're going to play," he tells Max.

Now Max is more interested in talking about baseball than Mary Ann's visit. But her visit is all I can think about. I'm going to cross the days off my cat calendar until she gets here. I really miss not having a best friend on my street.

We get in line to order at McDonald's. When it's my turn, I don't even hear the lady ask what I want.

"Earth to Mallory," says Max.

I order a Happy Meal and sit down. But my mind is definitely not on food.

Max sits down across from me. He has a Big Mac, a large order of fries, and a chocolate milk shake on his tray.

I watch him dip two French fries in his

milk shake. He stuffs them in his mouth. *Disgusting!* Even though my brain is busy planning my weekend with Mary Ann, watching Max makes me think of a joke.

"What's as long as California and wider than Texas?" I ask.

Max doesn't say *what* like he's supposed to. I give the answer anyway. "Your stomach! Get it?"

"Here's a question for you," Max says without laughing. "What's the only good thing about all the dumb stuff you do?"

I take a bite out of my cheeseburger and ignore Max.

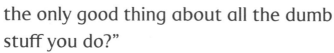

"We get to eat at McDonald's!" Max cracks up.

"Not funny," I say.

"News flash," says Max. "None of the dumb stuff you do is funny. So if you don't mind, lay off. I don't want the neighbors to think I have a total moron for a sister."

"Here's a news flash for you," I say to Max. "You're the only moron on our street." I take a sip of my Coke.

"Actually," I say to Max. "I don't know if you noticed, but the girl next door is a pretty big moron too."

Max sips his shake.

I stare at him. Max never sips his shake. He guzzles shakes. He slurps shakes. But he never ever sips them. That's when I get it: Max doesn't think the girl next door is a moron at all.

"You like Winnie!" I say. Now it's my

turn to crack up. This is even funnier than the jokes on my Happy Meal box.

"She's better than her brother," says Max. "Talk about a dumb kid."

"He's not dumb," I say. "He thought my jokes were hilarious."

"Shows what he knows." Max gets up to dump his tray in the trash.

Maybe Max is right about Joey. Maybe he's not. But it doesn't matter anyway. Mary Ann and I made a pinkie swear: *Never be friends with any boy next door.*

When I get home, I cross today off my calendar with a fat red marker. I draw a purple heart on the day Mary Ann is coming.

Just one month to go.

AN INVITATION

Ding-dong.

Ding-dong.

"Somebody get the door!" Dad shouts from upstairs.

I hop off the couch. It's our first official visitor, and I want to be the official greeter. I fling open the door.

Big mistake! It's Winnie with four things: a scowl on her face, Joey, and two bald guys.

Maybe Joey and the bald guys dragged

Winnie over to apologize to me. I saw a movie once where that happened.

The older bald guy hands me a bag. "Special delivery," he says.

What if there's something awful in the bag like a dead snake or a rat?

But I can tell by the smell it's not a dead snake or a rat. I open the bag and peek inside. Fresh hot bagels. Mmmm. I pick one and take a bite out of it. Double mmmm.

The younger bald guy talks first. "Hello, young lady," he says. "You've met my kids. I'm Winnie and Joey's dad, Mr. Winston, and this is my dad, Mr. Winston."

The older bald guy smiles. "You can call me Grandpa. Everybody does."

I take another bite out of my bagel. "I'm Mallory."

"Pleased to meet you, Mallory." Grandpa

shakes my bagel-free hand.

Mom comes up behind me and takes the bagel bag. "Mallory, don't be rude. Invite our guests in."

Dad comes downstairs, and the introductions start all over again.

Mr. Winston says he's sorry he hasn't come over sooner. Mom says we've been busy unpacking. Blah, blah, blah. For grown-ups who don't know each other, they have a lot to talk about.

Mom invites both Mr.Winstons in for coffee. Then she tells us kids to go play.

But we just stand there and look at each other. Don't grown-ups know that's what happens when they tell kids who don't know each other to go play?

"I'm going home," says Winnie. "I'm too old to

play." The front door slams behind her.

"Count me out." Max plops down on the couch. "I've got to do something really important, like finish this comic book."

That leaves Joey and me. I don't want to be friendly. But I don't want to be rude either. I take a bite out of my bagel.

"Want to see my room?"

"Lead the way," says Joey.

He follows me down the hall. It's hard to walk into my room because my scrapbooks are all over the floor. I push them into a pile in the corner to make room for both of us.

"It's a mess," I tell Joey. "We moved in

three days ago, and Mom says I have to have everything put away by the end of the week."

"No sweat," says Joey. "We moved in five years ago, and I still haven't finished putting my stuff away."

I think about Joey's mom. I wonder if Joey hasn't put his stuff away because he doesn't have a mom to tell him to do stuff like that. I feel bad just thinking about it.

But Joey doesn't look like he feels bad. He opens one of the joke books on my dresser. "What's another name for funny candy?" he asks.

I scratch my head. "I give up."

"Laughy taffy!"

"Ha-ha."

Joey closes the book. "You like jokes, don't you?"

"I used to," I tell him.

Joey looks at me like he's studying a long spelling word. "Were you upset the other day because Winnie didn't laugh at your jokes?"

Joey's pretty smart . . . for a boy.

"Yeah," I tell him. "I was a little mad at Winnie. But I was a lot mad at Max. He says everything I do is dumb."

"Your brother and my sister are going to get along great. Winnie thinks everything I do is dumb, too." Joey puts the joke book down. "It stinks, doesn't it?"

I roll my eyes. "Yeah, well what can we do?" Maybe no one's ever told Joey that big brothers and sisters get away with just about everything.

"We could give them a taste of their own medicine." He whispers like somebody is listening outside my door. "Play a joke on them. Something funny."

I look through my bookshelves. "Sorry," I tell him. "I can't find my copy of *Jokes to Play on Your Older Sibling.*"

Joey grins. "We don't need a book. We'll think up our own joke."

"Like what?" I can't imagine what we could do to Max and Winnie.

"Joey. . . . " His dad calls him from the other room. "We're leaving."

"To be continued," says Joey.

When we walk back into the den, the grown-ups are saying good-bye. "See you tonight," Mr. Winston says to Mom as he leaves.

"Seven sharp," says Grandpa Winston.

Dad waves and closes the door behind them.

"Where are we going at seven sharp?" I ask Mom.

"To the Winston's." Mom opens a box

marked Cookbooks. "We've been invited to a *welcome-to-the-neighborhood* barbecue. I have to think of something to bring."

"I know what you can leave at home," Max mumbles from behind his comic book.

Mom doesn't hear him. But I do. I know he means me, *and* I know he thinks I'm going to do something to embarrass him, *and* I don't care.

I've been invited to a party!

I'm going to make a scrapbook of my move to Fern Falls. I'm going to call it *My Moving Book*. It will be like my baby book and the first picture in it will be from tonight. On the top of the page, I'm going to write: *Me at my first party in the new neighborhood.*

I just hope when I'm a grown-up and I look back at *My Moving Book*, I'll be smiling in the first picture.

THE "NO JOKE" CLUB

Whenever I'm waiting for someone to open a door, I wonder if I have a booger in my nose. I try to think about other things, but my brain only lets me think about what might be in my nose.

The good news is I've never actually had a booger while I'm waiting.

The bad news is I feel like I do today. I bet Winnie answers her front door, sees it, and laughs so hard her head falls off.

But I get lucky. Joey answers the front door, and he doesn't even look at my nose. He just looks happy to see us. "Come in," he says. "We've been waiting for you."

We follow Joey into the backyard. Winnie is sitting in a chair reading a magazine. She doesn't even get up to say hello.

Mr. Winston and Grandpa come over to greet us. "Hey!" says Mr. Winston. He twirls the chef's hat on his head. "I hope you like chicken."

Mom and Dad tell Mr. Winston they love it.

I tell Mr. Winston I love chicken jokes.

"Chicken jokes, huh." Mr. Winston smiles. "I'd love to hear a chicken joke."

Max gives me one of his *don't-do-it* looks.

I ignore him. "Why did the chicken cross the road?"

"That's the oldest, dumbest joke on the planet," Winnie says without looking up from her magazine.

"To get to the other side." I ask the next joke before anyone has a chance not to laugh at my first one. "Does anybody know why the rooster crossed the road?"

"Why?" Joey asks.

"To show he wasn't a chicken."

Everybody laughs. Well . . . almost everybody. Winnie yawns, and Max doesn't move a muscle. I'm starting to think the best way to keep Max quiet is to keep him with Winnie. He doesn't say a word when she's around.

The grown-ups start talking.

"Want to see my room?" Joey asks me.

"Sure." I follow him through his house. I thought it would be a big mess. But I'm surprised. It's pretty neat.

We pass one room that's very neat. It's also very pink. I know without asking who it belongs to.

"I'm dead meat if I go in there," Joey tells me.

That doesn't surprise me a bit. I bet the president of the United States would need an invitation to go into Winnie's room.

Then we go into Joey's room. At least we try to. There's stuff everywhere. "Sit anywhere you can find a spot," Joey tells me.

I move a pile of T-shirts off a beanbag chair and sit down.

Joey sits on the floor. "Dad says I have to clean my room by the end of the summer, or I have to repeat second grade."

"Is he serious?" I can't believe a parent would say that.

Joey grins. "My dad loves to joke around. Me too. Speaking of jokes, I thought of a joke we can play on Winnie and Max."

"Huh?" I say. I can't believe he's serious.

Joey puts his finger to his lips and sticks his head out his door. He looks up and down the hall. "Want to hear my plan?" he asks softly.

I nod. Joey sits on the pile of T-shirts on the floor and whispers his plan to me. I know no one can hear because he's whispering so softly I can barely hear him.

When he finishes, I can't believe what I heard. I thought it would be impossible to think of something to do to Winnie and Max, but Joey's plan is great.

"We'll start a club," he says. "The 'No Joke' Club."

I frown. That sounds like the wrong name for this club to me. "Aren't we going to play jokes on Max and Winnie?"

"Sure," Joey says. "But we have to show them that treating us nice is NO joke."

I smile. "I get it."

"Joey. Mallory." Joey's dad calls us from the backyard. "Time for dinner."

"So when do we put our plan into action?" I ask Joey.

"We start tomorrow." He high-fives me. The "No Joke" Club is official.

We go outside in the backyard. Mr. Winston gives everyone big plates of barbecued chicken and baked beans.

I take a bite of chicken. Mmmm. "What do you call chicken that tastes good?"

"I hope delicious," says Mr. Winston.

"Finger lickin' chicken!" I take a bite and lick my lips.

"I'm glad you like it." Mr. Winston smiles.

Winnie rolls her eyes, and Max doesn't even look up from his plate. I know he thinks my joke is funny because I've heard him laugh when I've told it before.

But I also know he isn't planning to laugh today. Max must have a rule about it: absolutely no laughing or talking around Winnie.

While Mr. Winston clears the chicken plates, I make a note in my head: *tell Max he should find a better way to show girls he likes them.*

Mom cuts the cake she brought. Everyone eats a piece, and then we go home.

When I get in my room, I turn out my light and get right in bed.

Life on Wish Pond Road might not be so bad after all.

PAINTED
TOENAILS

I count red Xs on my calendar and force myself to do some math, even though it's summer break. The results are worse than I thought they would be.

It's been exactly two weeks, two days, fourteen hours, and twenty-two minutes since I promised Mary Ann I would write her a letter.

And I am going to write her. The problem is for the past two weeks, two days, fourteen hours, and twenty-two minutes, I've been very, very, very busy.

And I'm still very, very, very busy. I'm supposed to be at the wish pond this very minute for morning cat tricks.

I grab doughnuts with one hand and Cheeseburger with the other.

"C'mon!" Joey waves when he sees me coming down the street. "Cat trick lessons start promptly at nine."

I plop down on the rocks beside the wish pond and hand Joey a doughnut. He's very serious about cat trick lessons.

I am too. But so far, Cheeseburger doesn't seem to be much of a student. Last week, we tried to teach her how to shake paws. Once, she shook her tail. But she never even lifted a paw.

This week we are trying to teach her to roll over.

"OK," Joey says to Cheeseburger. "Watch Murphy." He holds the doughnut in the air in front of Murphy.

"Murphy, roll over." Murphy rolls over, and Joey gives him a little piece of a doughnut. I clap. "Your turn," he says to Cheeseburger.

Joey holds up a little piece of doughnut. Cheeseburger closes her eyes and stretches out on the rock.

"Maybe she's not in the mood for doughnuts," I say.

"We can't give up," says Joey. He claps his hands, and Murphy rolls over again.

"C'mon, Cheeseburger," says Joey. But Cheeseburger won't even open her eyes.

We spend the morning trying to keep Cheeseburger awake. I take my shoes off and stick my feet in the wish pond. It's getting hot out here.

Joey takes his shoes off too. "Maybe we should try again this afternoon after we skateboard."

Yikes. Joey and I always skateboard in the afternoons. He's been teaching me how to do it. But there won't be any skateboarding lessons for me today.

I tell Joey there's something I *have* to do.

When I get home, I shut my door and sit down at my desk. I write Dear Mary Ann on the top of a piece of paper.

Then I just sit at my desk. Writing letters is not as much fun as skateboarding.

But I have to write something. I
promised Mary Ann I would. The question
is what.

I take out another sheet of paper and
start over.

Dear Mary Ann,
I have something to tell you that I think
you will like hearing. You know what a
pain Max is, right?

Joey (my next-door neighbor) helped
me play a really funny trick on him. We
snuck into Max's room while he was still
sleeping and painted his toenails.

Can you believe it?

I did the actual painting while Joey held
his hand over my mouth. When we
finished, we crept back into my room and
burst out laughing. Max looked so funny.

When he woke up, he went nuts. (You know how nuts he can be.)

He was screaming and yelling. "GET THIS STUFF OFF OF ME! MALLORY, I'm GOING TO KILL YOU!"

He was hopping up and down and trying to wipe his toenails on my carpet. When he saw Joey (who he calls Kangaroo Boy, because he says a joey is the official name for a baby kangaroo), he yelled at him to hop back into his pouch.

You should have seen Max with sparkly purple toes. It was so funny!

We played a trick on Joey's sister (who is not nice...AT ALL!) too. One morning, Joey and I went into Winnie's bathroom while she was sleeping. We lifted up the toilet seat and stretched plastic wrap tight across the toilet. Then we put the seat down.

We hid in Joey's room and waited until we heard Winnie go into the bathroom.

When we heard her scream, we knew what had happened. Winnie came out of the bathroom, carrying her slippers. They were dripping wet with you-know-what. You should try this sometime (not to yourself, to someone else). It is so, so, so funny!

I can't wait for you to get here. G.2.G. (short for got to go). I'm late for skateboarding lessons.

Hugs and kisses!
Mallory

I reread my letter. In second grade, I learned there are three steps to writing a letter.

Step 1: Writing it.

Check.

Step 2: Rereading it.

Check.

Step 3: Mailing it.

There's no way I can do step three!

Joey and I have had a lot of fun since I moved in. But I think about the pinkie swear I made with Mary Ann. *I promise not to be friends with any boy next door.*

When Mary Ann reads my letter, she'll know I broke my pinkie swear. She won't be happy about that.

I don't know how I'm going to tell her I'm friends with Joey, but I do know writing it in a letter is a bad idea.

I rip up my letter. Then I look in my mirror and raise my right hand.

Tomorrow, I do solemnly swear to write Mary Ann.

A BAD MONTH

Dear Mary Ann,

I don't think letters are supposed to have titles. But if they did, I'd call this one A Bad Month.

Lots of bad things have happened since I moved to Fern Falls. I will tell you about them all.

Bad thing #1: My room is very, very, very small. Max got the big room, and I got the very, very, very small room.

Bad thing #2: My bathroom is not

actually my bathroom. It is the bathroom I have to share with max. (You'll have to share with him, too, when you come visit. But don't worry, we can lock him out. maybe we'll lock him out all day, and if he has to go really bad, he'll have to go in the backyard. Ha! Ha! Ha!)

Bad thing #3: my next door neighbor is a very mean girl. VERY, VERY, VERY MEAN! The only person who likes her is max (so you can imagine how mean she must be). She doesn't even talk to me except to tell me to leave her alone. YOU WON'T LIKE HER.

Bad thing #4: There's a wish pond on my street, but I don't think it works. Wishes are supposed to come true when you throw rocks into the pond. But I've been throwing them in since I moved

here, and none of my wishes have come
true. If they had, I would still be living
next door to you.

That's all there is to tell about me.
Everything was bad when I moved in a
month ago, and it hasn't gotten any
better since.

I can't wait to see you. We're going to
have so, so, so much fun. It will be just
like it used to be.

We'll paint our toenails. We'll take
Cheeseburger on long walks. We'll say

everything three times. We'll even play our favorite game (you know which one that is)!

I miss you so, so, so much! I am counting the days until you get here! (Max says he is too.)

Hugs! Hugs! Hugs! Kisses! Kisses! Kisses!

Mallory

I reread my letter. Even though I don't love, love, love writing letters, I think this one is good. I told Mary Ann about all the bad things that have happened to me since I moved here.

Then I think about what I *didn't* tell her. I didn't tell her that even though we made a pinkie swear not to be friends with the boy next door, I am.

I wrote in my letter that things will be just like they used to be. But I'm not sure how things with Mary Ann will be just like they used to be because now I'm friends with Joey, too.

All this thinking has given me a headache. I know why I don't like writing letters. You have to think about what you write in them, and I'm sick of thinking about what I've written in this one.

I put the letter to Mary Ann inside a purple envelope and lick it shut. I write S.W.A.K on the outside with a purple marker.

My letter to Mary Ann is sealed with a kiss, and it is on its way.

MALLORY IN THE MIDDLE

Dear Mallory,

I got your letter. I can't wait to see you!
I'm not writing much.

I'm going to see you so, so, so soon and
we can talk, talk, talk then.

We're going to have so much fun!

No one to bug us (except Max, of course!).

Just you and me. Just like old times.

Hugs! Hugs! Hugs! Kisses! Kisses! Kisses!

Mary Ann

There are three good reasons not to hide inside a curtain:

One. It's itchy.

Two. It's stinky.

Three. It's hard to read your mail.

I don't actually know why I'm trying to read Mary Ann's letter. I've read it so many times I've practically memorized it.

Especially the part about *just you and me, just like old times.*

When I lived next door to Mary Ann, it was just the two of us. But now I live next door to Joey. If I add up Mallory plus Mary Ann plus Joey, I get three.

And the bad thing about the number three is that someone is always in the middle. And I feel like that someone is going to be me.

I bend down to scratch my foot, but someone gets to it before I do.

"Gotcha!" Max pulls me out of my hiding spot. "How come you're not outside with Kangaroo Boy waiting for Birdbrain?"

Max laughs. "Those two animals should get along great."

I never talk to Max about my problems, but I could use some advice right now. "That's the problem," I tell him. "I haven't told Mary Ann I live next door to a boy who's my new friend. And I haven't told Joey my old best friend is coming to visit."

I look at Max. I hope he'll tell me what to do. And he does.

"Better get back inside those curtains."

Max laughs. "You're toast."

A car honks. Max is right. I am toast. Burned toast with no butter or jelly.

"C'mon." Max pulls me outside. "This visit might actually be fun."

I shove Mary Ann's letter in my pocket and run outside. Somehow I have to keep Mary Ann and Joey apart.

"MALLORY!" She runs to hug me. "I am so, so, so happy I'm here!"

I'm happy she's here too. I'm also happy Joey isn't outside in his front yard.

Our moms hug. Mary Ann's mom takes my mom by the arm, and they start walking into my house. "You have to show me absolutely everything," she says.

Mary Ann takes my arm. "Me too," she says. "I want to see everything."

"Mallory has a lot to show you," says Max.

I roll my eyes at him. He could probably get in the *Guinness Book of World Records* for Worst Older Brother.

"Wish pond first," says Mary Ann.

Mary Ann is usually full of good ideas, but this isn't one of them. If Joey sees us outside, he'll come too. I've got to keep Mary Ann inside.

I pull her by the hand. "House first."

I give her a tour of my room.

Then my house.

Then the closets in my house.

I want this tour to take as long as possible.

"Now for the kitchen drawers," I say. "You need to know where we keep the spoons in case you need a midnight snack and I'm asleep."

Mary Ann yawns. "This is boring. Let's go outside."

I've got to keep Mary Ann inside. I drag her back to my room. "There's something we have to do . . . it's toe time!" I sit down on the floor and start painting.

Mary Ann sits down and paints her toes too. As soon as all ten of hers are purple and shiny, she screws the top back on the bottle of polish. She stands up and slips on her flip-flops. "C'mon, I want to see the wish pond."

I put my toes carefully through the

fronts of my flip-flops. "Not so fast," I tell Mary Ann. "You don't want to mess up your polish."

I have a bad feeling about what she's going to find at the wish pond.

"Show me how it works," Mary Ann says when we get there. "I want to make a wish."

I pick up two rocks and hand one to Mary Ann. I want to make a wish too. But the moment I haven't been waiting for happens before I have a chance to wish it doesn't.

Joey walks out of his house and over to the wish pond.

"Hey, Mallory." Joey talks to me, but he's looking at Mary Ann. "Who's this? I've never seen her before."

I throw in my rock and make a quick wish. *I wish old friends and new friends can*

become instant friends.

I introduce my friends to each other. "Joey. Mary Ann. Mary Ann. Joey." I feel like they should shake.

"Mallory and I are best friends." Mary Ann smiles at Joey. "I'm visiting her for the weekend."

"Really?" Joey scratches his head like he's confused.

"Yes, really," says Mary Ann. "And we're going to have a great, great, great time because we're best, best, best friends. We lived next door to each other all our lives. Until she moved here, of course."

"Hmmm." Joey says *hmmm* like he's in math class trying to think of an answer he really doesn't know. "That's weird."

Mary Ann rolls her eyes. "What's so weird about that?"

Joey picks up a rock and throws it across

the pond. "It's weird that Mallory never told me you were coming to visit. I live next door to her. We play together every day, and she's never told me about you. I'm surprised. That's all."

I try to speak. But it's kind of hard when it feels like you've got a giant wad of gum stuck in your throat.

Mary Ann looks confused. "Who is this kid?"

I cross my freshly painted toes. I hope she understands.

I whisper in Mary Ann's ear so Joey can't hear me. "Even though we pinkie swore we wouldn't be friends with a boy next door, I have to play with Joey because I don't have anybody else to play with."

Mary Ann smiles. She looks like what I said makes sense to her.

Then I look at Joey. Max always tells me

boys don't care about secrets. But Joey
looks like he cares about the one I just
whispered to Mary Ann.

I lean over and whisper in Joey's ear.
"Mary Ann rode in a car for three hours to
come see me. While she's here, I have to
play with her. But when she leaves, we'll
play. OK?"

Joey picks up a rock and throws it across
the pond. "No," he says. "Not OK. Why
can't we all play?"

How do I tell Joey that's a bad idea?
Some people say having two friends means
double the fun. But I'm beginning to think
it means double the trouble.

"What a great idea!" says Mary Ann.
Joey can play with us."

Did I hear her right? Did Mary Ann say
Joey can play with us?

"Cool," says Joey.

Cool is right. I know why Mary Ann has been my best friend since I was born.

"So what are we going to play?" Joey asks.

"Mallory and I are going to teach you how to play our favorite game."

"Mega cool," says Joey. "I can't wait."

But I groan. This is not mega cool at all. I know the game we're going to play. It's my favorite game, and it's Mary Ann's favorite game.

But I don't think Joey's going to like it at all.

TASTER'S CHOICE

"OK," says Mary Ann. "Here's how you play."

She goes in the pantry and gets down boxes and bottles and jars. She goes to the refrigerator and brings out bowls and pitchers and plates.

When Mary Ann is finished, our kitchen table is covered with eggs, olives, peanut butter, pickles, sardines, gooseberry jelly, black licorice, biscuit dough, flour, butter, marshmallows, baking soda, lemon juice, leftover meat loaf, tuna fish, an onion, eggplant casserole, shredded coconut, frozen peas, coffee creamer, and prune juice.

Ick. When I look at some of the stuff on the table, I'm not sure why Mary Ann and I like this game. But we do.

In second grade, we played until we tasted everything in the kitchen. We even tasted some things from the bathroom like hand lotion and hair conditioner.

"Mallory, since you know how to play, you're first." Mary Ann takes the bandanna off her head and ties it around my eyes.

Then she explains the rules to Joey. "I'm going to spin Mallory around three times. Then she points to something on the table. Whatever she chooses, she has to taste. Then she has to guess what it is. Get it?"

"Got it," says Joey. "But what if you don't like what you taste?"

"Too bad," says Mary Ann. "That's how you play."

"OK," says Joey. "It can't be that bad. Right?"

"Right." Mary Ann giggles.

Wrong, I think to myself. I don't like the sound of Mary Ann's giggle.

She checks my blindfold and spins me. When I stop spinning, I point. I can't see, but I hear Mary Ann and Joey laughing. Not a good sign.

"Open up," says Mary Ann. She puts something cold and squishy in my mouth.

Ugh. Disgusting!

"Chew," Mary Ann says. "You know the rule." I do know the rule. *You have to eat the whole bite.* I wish I could spit this out though. I don't like cold, squishy foods.

"What is it?" asks Mary Ann.

It's not a marshmallow. It's not a sardine. "Eggplant casserole?" I guess.

"Right!" Mary Ann and Joey laugh. I rip off the blindfold and gulp down a glass of water. Whoever made up the recipe for eggplant casserole made a big mistake.

Mary Ann is next. She gets baking soda.

My Aunt Sally used to put baking soda on my cousin Caroline when she had diaper rash. Anything that cures diaper rash must taste even worse than eggplant.

When it's Joey's turn, he gets frozen peas.

"Cold," he says after he makes his guess.

"But not too bad."

We play until we taste almost everything on the table. I get some really gross stuff. Flour, biscuit dough, and butter.

"Knock, knock," I say when I get butter.

"Who's there?" Mary Ann asks.

"Butter."

"Butter who?"

"Butter hope you get something that tastes better than butter."

Mary Ann laughs at my joke, but she doesn't get anything better. She gets some of the worst foods on the table. Prune juice, an onion, and leftover meat loaf.

Joey gets a marshmallow, peanut butter,

and black licorice. It's time to stop this game before someone gets something really gross. "Who wants to play outside?" I ask.

"One more round," says Mary Ann.

"OK by me," says Joey.

I don't know if it's the butter, the biscuit dough, or the idea of another round, but my stomach hurts. The blindfold goes back on. I get gooseberry jelly.

Mary Ann gets lemon juice.

When it's Joey's turn, Mary Ann blindfolds him and spins him really fast. When he points, his finger misses the table and points to something in the pantry.

The something

he's pointing to is Cheeseburger's cat food. Mary Ann covers her mouth to keep from laughing and takes a pellet out of the bag.

"NO!" I mouth to Mary Ann. But she pops the pellet in Joey's mouth before I can stop her. I cover my eyes. This is exactly what I didn't want to happen.

Joey chews. "UGH! DOUBLE UGH! TRIPLE, QUADRUPLE UGH!" He runs to the sink and spits. "It tastes like crunchy tuna fish."

"Guess again." Mary Ann starts laughing.

Joey rips the blindfold off. "I don't know what it is, but I'm going to be sick." He drinks straight from the faucet. "What was that?"

Mary Ann holds up the bag of cat food.

Joey stares at her. "You fed me cat food?"

Mary Ann is on the floor, she's laughing

so hard. I don't make a sound. I don't want Joey to think I had anything to do with this.

But Joey looks right at me. "How could you let me eat cat food?"

I try to explain that he pointed to it. That's how you play the game. That Mary Ann fed it to him . . . not me!

But the flour I ate must have turned into glue because my mouth is stuck shut.

"I thought you were my friend. Friends don't let friends eat cat food." Joey spits in the sink again. He stares at me. "I wish you didn't live next door to me!"

"Maybe your wish will come true," says Mary Ann.

But Joey doesn't stick around to find out how. The back door slams behind him.

Somehow, I knew this was going to be trouble. Part of me feels like I should run after Joey and part of me feels like I want to stay here with Mary Ann.

All of me feels like the cream filling inside an Oreo must feel when the cookie is pulled apart.

Two sides want me, and I don't know who to stick to.

MALLORY
IN A BOX

I never thought I wanted to see another box. But now I'm inside one on the way to Mary Ann's house, and no one even knows I'm gone.

I think back to Friday afternoon.

Mary Ann and I were in the kitchen trying to scrape dried biscuit dough off the counter when she told me her plan.

"NO WAY!" I shouted. "It'll never work."

"Of course it will." Then she got a piece

of paper and made a list of all the reasons I should come live with her.

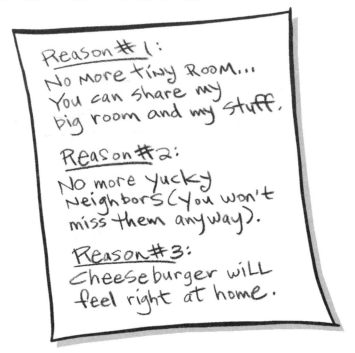

Reason #1:
No more tiny Room...
You can share my
big room and my stuff.

Reason #2:
No more yucky
Neighbors (You won't
miss them anyway).

Reason #3:
Cheeseburger will
feel right at home.

I read her list. Then I made my own list, in my head, of all the reasons I should stay where I am.

Reason #1: My room is tiny, but it has all *my* stuff in it.

Reason #2: Only one of my neighbors is yucky (I will miss the other one).

Reason #3: Cheeseburger will miss her cat trick lessons.

I spent the whole weekend telling Mary Ann why her plan wouldn't work.

She spent the whole weekend trying to convince me that it would.

We were still in our sleeping bags this morning, and Mary Ann was still trying to get me to go along with what she had in mind.

"It's simple," she said for the ten-millionth time. "There's an empty box in the back of the van. When it's time for us to leave, just make sure no one is looking, and get in it. That's all you have to do."

"What happens when my mom and dad find out I'm gone?" I asked her for the ten-millionth time. "Then I'll be in trouble. BIG, BIG, BIG TROUBLE!"

"How can you get in trouble if they can't find you?" Mary Ann got out of her sleeping bag and sat on my dresser. She crossed her arms. "Anyway, you owe it to me. You broke your pinkie swear. You said you'd never be friends with any boy next door."

It made me mad that Mary Ann didn't understand that I didn't have a choice. "Who else was I going to play with?" I crossed my arms. "Max?"

Mary Ann thought for a minute. "Well, maybe you didn't have a choice," she said.

"It wasn't like you had me next door anymore. But now you do have a choice. You can follow my plan."

I didn't know what to say to that. Plus, riding in a box for three hours wasn't exactly my idea of fun.

"How do you know I'll fit in the box?" I asked Mary Ann.

"It's a big box," she said. "And once we get to my house, it'll be worth it. We'll be best friends like we used to be. Except even better because you'll be living with me."

Part of me wanted to go and part of me wanted to stay. I still wasn't sure which part I wanted to listen to, when Mary Ann said it was time to put our plan into action.

"Hurry!" she said. "I hear my mom telling your mom and dad good-bye."

"But I'm still in my pj's," I told Mary Ann.

She opened my window. "You've got to go now!"

And without another thought, I climbed out with Cheeseburger and got in the box in the van.

I could hear everyone come outside. I couldn't see, but I heard lots of good-byes and thank-yous.

Then I heard the words that made my heart beat so loudly I was sure someone would discover me.

"Where's Mallory?" asked Mom. "I know she'll want to say good-bye."

I thought I was toast for sure. But then Mary Ann said, "We already said good-bye. We stayed up all night talking. Mallory's taking a nap."

She whispered the part about the nap like she didn't want to wake me up.

Then Mom said I'd made a good choice,

and the next thing I knew, we were off. Good-bye Wish Pond Road.

Hello box . . . hot, small, scratchy box. I try to think of things I can do inside this box for the next three hours.

But all I can think of are things I can't do.

I can't sing.

I can't sneeze.

I can't even go to the bathroom.

I try to think about all the fun Mary Ann and I are going to have when we get to her house, but my brain keeps thinking about all the things I won't be able to do.

I won't be able to stick my feet in the wish pond.

I won't be able to be in The "No Joke" Club.

I won't even be able to fight with Max.

I can hear Mom's words. *I'd made a good choice.*

Even though I really want to be with Mary Ann, I feel like I've made some not-so-good choices. Like leaving home in this box. Like letting Mary Ann feed Joey the cat food. I should have stopped her.

The more I think about it, the worse I feel. If I did to myself what I did to Joey, I wouldn't even be my own friend.

I bet that cat food tasted really gross. Just like the inside of this box smells.

I move my legs and try to get comfortable. But that's not so easy to do when you're cooped up inside a smelly box with nothing to do but think about your choices.

I look at my watch. Two hours and thirty-three minutes to go.

I remember what Mary Ann said. *Once we get to my house, it'll all be worth it.*

I hope she's right.

I look at Cheeseburger who is asleep on my lap. Nothing seems to be bothering her. Cats are lucky. They don't have to make choices.

Even though I wouldn't want to eat cat food, sometimes I think it would be a whole lot easier to be a cat.

NEVER COMING OUT

"I'm not going back, and you can't make me!"

Dad isn't listening to one word I've said. He might as well be dragging me by my hair like a cave girl.

I dig my heels into the gravel in Mary Ann's driveway. "I don't want to go back to Fern Falls!" I yell. "I want to stay here and live with Mary Ann."

At least . . . I think I do.

I had fun living with Mary Ann. Even if it was only for five hours and thirty-three minutes. We did a lot of things Mary Ann and I love to do. We ate cold pizza for lunch. We looked at old scrapbooks we made together. We made up a list of secret passwords in case we ever need them.

But there were a lot of things I like doing with Joey that I didn't get to do when I lived with Mary Ann . . . like going to the wish pond and skateboarding and playing with Murphy and Cheeseburger.

But still, I went to a lot of trouble to get here, and I'm not ready to go back yet.

I hold tight to Cheeseburger and hide behind Mary Ann. "We're not leaving!"

Dad reaches behind Mary Ann and grabs my arm. "I'm sorry," he says to Mary Ann's mom. "Get in the car young lady. You've got some explaining to do" is what he says to me.

As soon as I buckle my seat belt, Dad starts with questions.

Did I realize that I ran away from home?

Did I care that he and Mom were worried about me?

Did I think I could live at Mary Ann's house?

Did I know he would have to drive six hours to get me and bring me home?

Did I consider anyone's feelings other than my own?

I cross my arms. What about how I feel?

I felt weird when we got to Mary Ann's house and she said to me, "You're home." When I looked out her window at what used to be my home, it didn't look like my home anymore. It wasn't even the same color as it was when it was mine.

When Mary Ann and I were next-door neighbors, it was easy to be best friends. Now it's hard because everything is different.

"Earth to Mallory," Dad says. "I'm waiting for some answers."

But I have questions of my own.

"Why can't I live in one place with all the people I like and do all the things I like doing?" I kick the back of Dad's seat. "It's not fair."

Dad looks back at me in the mirror. His face is serious.

"Mallory, things change. I know moving hasn't been easy for you. But Mary Ann will

always be your friend. You don't live in the same place anymore, and it's important for both of you to make new friends."

This isn't what I want to hear. I wish Dad would say something like, *"Mallory, honey, we're sorry we ever made you move. We know this has been hard for you and we feel awful about it. We want to make it up to you somehow. We'll do anything. Even give away Max."*

But that's not what Dad says.

"Running away from home was wrong," says Dad. "We didn't know where you were. We looked everywhere. We were worried about you. We love you very much."

I cross my hands in my lap. Dad always says stuff like that when he's mad at me. It would make things a lot easier if he would say, *"Mallory, we hate you very much."* Then I could say, "I hate you very much" right back.

But now I don't know what to say. I scratch behind my ear. "I'm sorry," I mumble to Dad in the front seat.

"Apology accepted," says Dad. "I think we've cleared the air."

Not totally. There's one thing I still want to know. "Dad," I ask. "How did you know where I was?"

"Thankfully, Joey had the good sense to tell us he saw you get into the van."

My face feels hot. Did I hear Dad right? How could Joey tell on me?

"Joey did the right thing," says Dad. "I'm proud of him."

Proud of him? How can my Dad be proud of a rat?

Mary Ann should have fed him rat food, not cat food. When I see him, I'm going to feed him some. How could he give away my secret?

Dad and I ride the rest of the way without saying anything. I try counting trees to make the time pass. But I stop when I get to 1,062. I've spent a lot of time in a car lately, and this ride is making me sick.

Dad pulls into the driveway. "Home sweet home," he says. But I don't say a word. Part of me is kind of glad I'm back on Wish Pond Road. Part of me wishes I wasn't.

Mom and Max are waiting for me on the front porch.

"Too bad," says Max as I get out of the car. "I was just getting used to being an only child."

"Max, not today," says Mom. She tries to hug me, but I run past her to my room. I slam my door and lay down on the bed.

I cover my head with my pillow. I want to be left alone, but I hear something.

Knock. Knock.

"Mallory, open the door."

I shove my fingers in my ears.

Knock. Knock. Knock.

"C'mon, Sweet Potato," says Mom.

"I'm not opening my door."

Knock. Knock. Knock. Knock. Knock.

"Go away! I don't feel like talking."

Mom and Dad whisper to each other. "Maybe we should leave her for a while," says Dad. "She knows what she did."

I hear them walking down the hall. I curl up on the bed next to Cheeseburger and stare out the window.

I'll leave with Cheeseburger. Mary Ann can come with us. We'll live at Disney World. We'll never go to school. We'll eat all the junk food we want. Nobody will be able to tell us what to do.

It's a lot to think about. I roll over and close my eyes.

When I hear a knock on my door, I rub my eyes and look outside. It's almost dark. I've been asleep for a while.

"Mallory," Mom says softly. "Dinnertime."

I turn on my light. Then I remember. "No

dinner for me." I lie back down on the bed.

"Knock, knock," says Mom.

I don't answer.

Mom tries again. "Knock, knock."

"Who's there?" I play along because I know Mom won't stop unless I do.

"Olive."

I know this joke. "Olive who?"

"Olive you," says Mom.

"I have a joke for you," I tell Mom.

"I would love to hear it," Mom says.

"What has red hair, freckles, and is really, really, really miserable?"

Mom doesn't say *what*. I open my door and finish my joke anyway. "ME! I am really, really, really miserable. And I don't want

ME → (MiSERabLe)

dinner. What I want is to make a wish, and I want it to come true."

Mom looks at me for a long time like I'm a tricky question on a crossword puzzle. "Mallory," she finally says. "Why don't you take a walk to the wish pond?"

"What for? If I throw in a million rocks, I don't think my wish will come true."

"Well, it certainly won't come true if you stay locked up in your room," Mom says.

"Fine, fine, fine." I walk out the door and head toward the wish pond.

But if my wish doesn't come true this time, I'm calling a wish pond repairman.

WISHES COMING TRUE

I sit down on the edge of the wish pond, pick up a rock, and throw it in. *I wish things never had to change.*

I dig my fingers through the rocks on the edge of the pond. There are red rocks and gray rocks and white rocks. There are big rocks and little rocks and flat rocks. There are lots of rocks, which is a good thing because I have lots of wishes.

Something catches my eye. It's a teeny,

tiny black pebble, but it's very shiny. When I pick it up, it feels warm and smooth in my hand. Something about this rock feels special.

I close my eyes. *I wish* . . .

But I don't finish. Someone sits down beside me.

"You're back," says Joey.

I open my eyes. "Thanks to you. Otherwise I would have been gone for good." I put my shiny black pebble on the ground and cross my arms.

"Hey, where did you find this?" Joey picks up my pebble.

"Give it back!" I grab it out of his fingers.

"It's yours," Joey says. "A wish pebble only works for the person who finds it."

A wish pebble. I've never heard of a wish pebble. I don't feel like having a conversation with Joey, but I want to know what he's talking about.

"What's a wish pebble?"

"You don't know?" Joey seems surprised. "Everyone on this street knows about wish pebbles."

"I haven't lived here that long. Remember?"

"These shiny black ones are wish pebbles," Joey says. They're rare and hard to find. I've searched through these rocks since I moved here and never found one. You're lucky."

I turn the pebble over. "What's so special about a wish pebble?"

Joey laughs. "When you make a wish with a wish pebble, your wish is supposed to come true."

I think about the Legend of the Wish Pond. Maybe the farmer's wife found three wish pebbles. This wish is important. I squeeze my pebble.

"Go ahead," says Joey. "Throw it in. But make sure you wish for what you really want."

"Shhh," I say. "I can't wish while you're talking."

I close my eyes. *I wish things never had to change.* I squeeze the pebble in the palm of my hand. I'm ready to throw my wish pebble in the pond.

"Know what?" Joey says.

I hold on to my pebble and open one eye. It's hard to make a wish when you're interrupted. "What now?"

"I'm glad you're back. When you left, I came down here and looked for a wish pebble. I tried to wish you back. But I couldn't find a wish pebble so that's why I told your parents."

Joey picks up a plain gray rock and throws it into the pond. "Wish Pond Road was no fun without you."

I close my eye. Even though I don't like that Joey told on me, I do like living on Wish Pond Road and being friends with Joey.

I squeeze the pebble in my hand. Then I change my wish.

I wish I could be friends with Mary Ann and Joey. I throw my wish pebble into the pond and wait for something to happen.

And it does. I get a feeling . . . a feeling that my pinkie swear doesn't matter anymore . . . a feeling that I can be friends with Mary Ann and Joey . . . a feeling that my wish is coming true.

I open my eyes and smile. "Hey, Joey, want to hear a joke?"

He nods.

"Knock, knock."

"Who's there?"

"Ima."

"Ima who?"

"Ima sorry I fed you cat food."

Now it's Joey's turn to smile. "That's OK. I kind of liked it. But next time, I'm going to try it with ketchup."

"DISGUSTING!" I lean over into the wish pond. "I think I'm going to puke!"

"Gotcha!" says Joey. "But next time we play, I go first."

"I don't know about that!" What I do know is that if I don't get home for dinner, I'll be in big trouble. And I've been in enough trouble for one day.

I open the front door and take a deep breath. Something smells terrific. I head straight for the kitchen. Mom, Dad, and Max are eating Chinese food.

I'm so hungry, I skip the chopsticks and pick up a fork.

Mom and Dad look at each other but don't say a thing. When I'm done, Max hands me a fortune cookie.

"I saved it for you," he says.

I open it and unroll my fortune. *No need to worry. Good times ahead for you on Wish Pond Road.*

There's something fishy about this fortune. I look at Max. He's trying not to smile.

I pop my cookie in my mouth. Then I hand him the fortune. "You'll have to save this for someone who needs it," I tell him.

I'm not worried a bit.

Dear Mary Ann,

How are you? I'm fine...NOW! But I wasn't when I left your house. Boy was I in big trouble. You should have heard Dad in the car. (Actually, you're lucky you didn't have to!)

He was VERY, VERY, VERY MAD that I ran away from home. I won't go into the whole thing, but the whole way home he was like Mallory this and Mallory that.

Mallory, Mallory, Mallory. Running away from home was wrong, wrong, wrong.

I wanted to explain to Dad that I knew running away from home was wrong. That you've always been my best friend. That I didn't want you to think I broke our pinkie swear.

But then Dad said, "Mallory, things change. Mary Ann will always be your friend. You don't live in the same place anymore, and it's important for both of you to make new friends."

And then I didn't say much. I didn't know what to say.

I went to the wish pond to wish that things never had to change. But I guess Dad is right. Things do change, and we both have to make new friends. It makes me sad that we can't live next door to each other and be best friends every day.

But I have a great, great, great idea. Next time you visit, we'll go to the wish pond and make a wish together.

We'll wish that one day we can live next door to each other.

Just think how much fun we'll have! We'll do everything together. We'll chew the same kind of gum. We'll paint our

toenails the same color, and we'll say everything three times!
   Hugs! Hugs! Hugs!
   Kisses! Kisses! Kisses!
   mallory

   P.S. mom says you can visit again soon. I asked, "How soon?" She said, "Very soon!" And I said, "Unless it's tomorrow, it's not soon enough for me!"
   P.P.S. Friends-4-ever-and-ever-and-ever!